A Road Might Lead to Anywhere

by Rachel Field   Illustrated by Giles Laroche

Little, Brown and Company

Boston · Toronto · London

Also by Giles Laroche

GENERAL STORE
by Rachel Field

SING A SONG OF PEOPLE
by Lois Lenski

First Edition

"A Road Might Lead to Anywhere" was first published under the
title "Roads" in a collection of poetry entitled *The Pointed People*
by Rachel Field, copyright 1924 by Yale University Press, copyright
renewed 1952 by Arthur S. Pederson. This edition is reprinted by
arrangement with Macmillan Publishing Company, a division of
Macmillan, Inc.

Library of Congress Cataloging-in-Publication Data

Field, Rachel, 1894–1942.
   A road might lead to anywhere/by Rachel Field; illustrated by
Giles Laroche.
       p.   cm.
   Summary: After reading about faraway lands, a young girl closes
her eyes and imagines all the wonderful places a road could take
her, from a cave full of treasure to a witch's house and even to
Mexico.
   ISBN 0-316-28178-6
   [1. Roads — Fiction. 2. Travel — Fiction.] I. Laroche, Giles,
ill. II. Title.
PZ7.F475Ro   1990   89-32815
[E] — dc20   CIP
                                                          AC

10 9 8 7 6 5 4 3 2 1

WOR

Published simultaneously in Canada by
Little, Brown & Company (Canada) Limited

Printed in the United States of America

For C.B.B.

G.L.

A road might lead to anywhere—

To harbor towns and quays,

Or to a witch's pointed house

Hidden by bristly trees.

It might lead past the tailor's door,

Where he sews with needle and thread,

Or by Miss Pim the milliner's,

With her hats for every head.

It might be a road to a great, dark cave
With treasure and gold piled high,

Or a road with a mountain tied to its end,
Blue-humped against the sky.

Oh, a road might lead you anywhere—
To Mexico

or Maine.

But then, it might just fool you, and—

Lead you back home again!

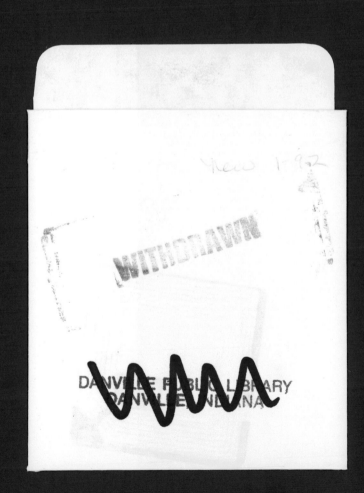